The Perfect CLUBHOUSE

by Daniel J. Mahoney

Clarion Books • New York

Clarion Books
a Houghton Mifflin Company imprint
215 Park Avenue South, New York, NY 10003
Copyright © 2004 by Daniel J. Mahoney

The illustrations were executed in acrylic gouache.
The text was set in 14-point Journal.

www.houghtonmifflinbooks.com

Printed in Singapore

Library of Congress Cataloging-in-Publication Data

Mahoney, Daniel J.,
The perfect clubhouse / by Daniel J. Mahoney.
p. cm.
Summary: When four friends decide to build the perfect clubhouse, they quickly discover
that each has a different idea about what is perfect.
ISBN 0-618-34672-4
[1. Clubhouses—Fiction. 2. Cooperativeness—Fiction.
3. Friendship—Fiction.] I. Title.
PZ7.M27685Pe 2004
[E]—dc22   2003011463

TWP 10 9 8 7 6 5 4 3 2 1

For Marissa and Alex

One summer morning, Stanley invited his friends Heston, Floyd, and Julius over to work on some science experiments. They were having a great time when Stanley's mom discovered them.

"Stanley Bartholomew! What did I tell you about conducting science experiments in the house?" she said.

"But, Mom," protested Stanley, "we're pushing back the frontiers of knowledge."

"Push them back outside," she said, pointing to the door.

5

6

"Now where do we go?" asked Stanley.

"We can't go to my house," said Heston. "My mom is going to have her baby soon, and she needs peace and quiet."

"My house is out, too," said Julius. "The minute we got there, my little sisters would start bothering us."

"I'd invite everyone to my apartment," said Floyd, "but it's too small for any real fun."

The four friends were glum. They needed a place to call their own.

"Hey, I have an idea," said Floyd. He took a well-worn Superdog comic from his back pocket and opened it to the last page. "Check out this cool clubhouse you can order. It comes with a secret escape hatch and a night-vision telescope so you can see if there are any monsters sneaking around in the dark."

"Maybe if we combine all our money we can buy it," said Julius.

They emptied their pockets onto the picnic table.

Julius added up their money. Clearly, they did not have enough.

"Wait a minute," said Heston. "My dad just added on a room for the new baby, and there's plenty of lumber left over. We can build our own clubhouse!"

"Perfect!" said his friends.

Heston, Julius, and Floyd dashed over to Heston's house and returned with the supplies. They found Stanley by the garden.

"This is the perfect spot for our clubhouse," Stanley said. "If we put it here, we can study the corn borers and slugs and cutworms that eat the vegetables."

"Looks good to me," said Julius. "I love vegetables."

Just then Stanley's mom called him in for lunch. "Sorry, I have to go," said Stanley. "Let's meet back here in an hour."

13

When Julius, Floyd, and Heston returned, there was no sign of Stanley—or the supplies. "Maybe he was abducted by aliens," said Floyd. "That happened to Superdog once."

They finally found Stanley by the pond. "This is an even better place for our clubhouse," he said. "We can do experiments with fish eggs and duckweed and pond scum."

"Looks good to me," said Heston. "When we camp out in the clubhouse, we can take an early-morning swim."

They spent the afternoon working together on their clubhouse. At supper time, they stopped for the day.

"Wow! It looks really great," said Heston.

His friends agreed. All of them felt very proud of what they'd done, and they decided to meet the next morning to finish the job.

When Floyd, Julius, and Heston arrived the next day, the clubhouse was gone. Julius sighed. "*Now where did Stanley move it?*" he said.

"Hey, guys." It was Stanley, calling from a small clearing in the woods. "I dragged the clubhouse over here so we can study leaf mold and mushrooms and decaying stuff. This is *definitely* the best place to put it."

"Looks good to me," said Floyd. "The trees will give us cover to hide from bad guys, monsters, and aliens."

SCIENCE

↑ UP

"Let's get started," said Stanley. "I brought a boxful of science equipment from my house so we can set up the lab."

"I see," said Floyd.

"I'm going to paint the inside of the clubhouse," said Julius, pulling out some brushes.

"Oh," said Stanley.

"I plan to build a fire pit for our camp-outs," said Heston, uncovering a pile of stones in his wagon.

"Hmm," said Julius.

"I've got all sorts of gadgets to spy-proof the clubhouse," said Floyd. "Also several masks and capes."

"Really?" said Heston.

They all set to work, but this time they each worked alone.
Floyd fastened a big antenna to the roof. "That should do it," he
said. "Now we can pick up radio signals from enemy agents."

"Wait a minute," said Heston. "I was going to put a lookout tower there, so we could see the stars when we camp out at night."

"Okay," said Floyd. "I'll attach the antenna to a tree instead."

"You can't," said Stanley. "Then we won't be able to move the clubhouse."

"Who says we're moving it?" said Floyd. "This is the perfect spot."

"I liked the place by the garden better," said Julius.

"I liked the place by the pond better," said Heston.

The four friends frowned at each other.

PAINT

PAINT

"Never mind," Julius said at last. "Come and see what I've done inside."
Heston, Floyd, and Stanley ducked into the clubhouse and looked
around. They couldn't believe their eyes.

"It looks like a supermarket in here," said Stanley.

"Yes," said Julius. "Isn't it wonderful?"

"Not really," said Floyd. "It doesn't look like a superhero clubhouse
at all."

24

"That's because it isn't one," snapped Julius. "It's an art studio."

"An art studio!" exclaimed Stanley. "No way! This clubhouse is a science lab. I've got all my equipment set up so we can do experiments."

"Forget experiments," said Heston. "What I want to do is roast marshmallows and tell ghost stories and have a camp-out."

The four friends were furious with each other.

Stanley stomped off to work in his lab.

Julius started another painting.

26

Heston told himself a ghost story.

Floyd put on a mask and cape and went looking for bad guys.

No one was happy.

Finally, Julius spoke up. "You know what, Heston?" he said. "Toasted marshmallows sound pretty good to me. I like your idea of a camp-out."

"And I like your idea of an art studio," said Heston. "Painting looks like fun."

"A science lab could be really cool," Floyd said to Stanley. "Maybe we can find an alien to do experiments on."

"Sure," replied Stanley. "But we'll probably need to dress up like superheroes to catch one."

"I guess our clubhouse can be anything we want it to be," said Julius.

"Yes," said Stanley. "All we have to do is move it one last time."

Together, they dragged the clubhouse to the middle of the yard, so it was equal distance from the garden, the pond, and the woods.

29

They spent the rest of the day painting pictures,

conducting experiments,

and playing superheroes.

That night they had a camp-out.

"This really *is* the perfect clubhouse," said Floyd.

"Perfect," agreed Heston and Julius.

Stanley said nothing. He was staring up into the trees.

"Stanley," said Julius, "don't *you* think it's perfect?"

"What? Oh, yes," said Stanley. "I was just wondering . . . wouldn't it be even more perfect as a treehouse?"